Fairy Bears

Misty

 "I promise to do my best. I promise to work hard to care for the world and all its plants, animals and children. This is the Fairy Bear Promise."

Look out for more magical Fairy Bears!

Dizzy

Sunny

Blossom

Sparkle

Primrose

Misty

Lulu

Poppy

Visit the secret world of the Fairy Bears and
explore the magical Crystal Caves . . .

www.fairybearsworld.com

Fairy Bears
Misty

Julie Sykes

Illustrated by Samantha Chaffey

MACMILLAN CHILDREN'S BOOKS

First published 2010 by Macmillan Children's Books
a division of Macmillan Publishers Limited
20 New Wharf Road, London N1 9RR
Basingstoke and Oxford
Associated companies throughout the world
www.panmacmillan.com

ISBN 978-0-330-51206-0

1 3 5 7 9 8 6 4 2

A CIP catalogue record for this book is available from
the British Library.

Printed and bound in the UK by CPI Mackays, Chatham ME5 8TD

For Antonia, who was there
when I found my first Fairy Bear

Firefly Meadow
Sycamore
GRAND DOOR
Caves for Fairy Bears who work for King & Queen
Turquoise Chamber
Diamond Arch
To The Royal Caves
ROYAL TUNNEL
MAIN TUNNEL
Whispering Pool
Rocky Island
Rowing Lake
Honey Bridge

Tree
Firefly Meadow
Nectar Cave
Diamond Dell
Starlight Cave
Crystal Maze
Ruby Grotto
Hospital Cave
School Caves
Air Ball Stadium
To The Home Caves
Play park
Underground Stream
To Royal Theatre

Prologue

At the bottom of Firefly Meadow, not far from the stream, stands a tall sycamore tree. The tree is old with a thick grey trunk and spreading branches. Hidden amongst the branches is a forgotten squirrel hole. If you could fly through the squirrel hole and down the inside of the tree's hollow trunk, you would find a secret door that leads to a special place. Open the door and step inside the magical Crystal Caves, home of the Fairy Bears.

The Fairy Bears are always busy. They work hard caring for nature and children everywhere. You'll have to be quick to see them, and you'll have to believe in magic.

1

Fairy Bears

Do you believe in Fairy Bear magic?
Can you keep a secret? Then come on
in – the Fairy Bears would love to meet
you.

Chapter One

The moment Misty the Fairy Bear
arrived in the school playground she was
surrounded by a crowd of her friends.

"Hi, everyone," she said. "Primrose and
I had a brilliant idea. We thought we'd go
to the underground lake after school. Who
wants to come with us?"

"Me!" everyone shouted noisily.

The underground lake was a popular
place to visit. Misty loved going there to dip
her paws in the water, fly over to Rocky
Island or row in the magical boats that

were charmed so they couldn't capsize.

Misty's eyes sparkled happily.

"Great. It'll be really good fun if you all come along."

The school bell sounded and the Fairy Bears fluttered to the door. As they crossed the playground, Misty noticed Coral walking indoors on her own. Impulsively she flew over to her and said, "Hi, Coral. Some of us are going to the underground lake after school today. Would you like to come too?"

Coral seemed surprised by the invite.

"Thanks, Misty, but I can't. I promised to help Mum polish Queen Tania's jewels when I get home."

Coral's parents worked for the Fairy Bear King and Queen and Coral often helped them.

"Another time then," said Misty.

4

"Yes, I'd like that," said
Coral shyly.

As Coral flew
indoors, Primrose
turned to Misty.

"That was nice of
you to ask her to come
with us."

Coral wasn't very popular with the other
Fairy Bears because she often said unkind
things.

Misty shrugged.

"It seemed mean to leave her out. Coral's
all right when you get to know her."

"You get on with everyone," laughed
Primrose.

Misty and her friends chattered excitedly
about their trip to the lake as they entered
the class cave. Miss Alaska followed them in
and immediately the class fell silent. Misty's

blue wings and pale gold fur tingled with excitement when she saw the sycamore leaf in Miss Alaska's paw. Was it someone else's turn to go and do a task? Misty glanced around the class trying to guess who would be chosen.

"Good morning!" Miss Alaska smiled at the silent Fairy Bears. "Today it's Misty's turn to take her first task. Let's say the Fairy Bear Promise and then I'll tell her what the task is."

Misty leaped out of her seat and grabbed paws with Primrose and Lulu. Her heart was pounding so loudly she was surprised no one could hear it. Closing her brown eyes she tried to concentrate on the Fairy Bear Promise, but, knowing she was about to go on her first task, made it difficult. The tasks were very important. They involved leaving the Crystal Caves to help someone or the environment they lived in. Often the problem was solved using Fairy Bear magic. Junior Fairy Bears had to pass all their tasks before they could move up into the seniors.

"I promise to do my best. I promise to work hard to care for the world and all its plants, animals and children. This is the Fairy Bear Promise," chanted Misty. She opened her eyes and took the leaf from Miss Alaska, reading it quickly.

"It says that I must visit a girl called Jessica and help her to make friends with her new stepsister, Becky." Misty's blue wings fluttered thoughtfully as she read the task again. Why was Jessica finding it hard to

make friends with her new sister? Misty
didn't understand. She was an only Fairy
Bear and would have loved a sister or a
brother to play with. Picking up her golden
wand, with a star-shaped sapphire set in
the end, Misty went to look in the magic
mirror to see if it would give her any clues
about her task. As she peered into the
rectangular-shaped glass, the tiny crystals
round the frame sparkled brightly. At first
her reflection stared back then in a swirl of
blue mist the picture faded and Misty saw a
young girl with shoulder-length blonde hair
pushing her fringe out of her eyes as she put
on a riding hat. When the hat was fastened,
the girl untied a pretty palomino pony from
outside a stable and nimbly mounted it.
A smaller girl with wavy brown hair and
hazel eyes stood watching her.

"That must be Becky," whispered Misty.

Jessica waved at Becky then rode her
pony away, leaving Becky standing alone.
A bicycle was propped against the fence.
A cycle helmet with Jessica's name written

on the strap hung from the handlebars. Becky looked as if she might get on the bike, but, shaking her head sadly, she went inside the stable. The picture flickered and disappeared, leaving Misty's indignant reflection staring back at her. Poor Becky! Why had Jessica left her alone like that? She could have easily lent Becky her bicycle so that Becky could have gone too.

"Oh dear!" said Coral, looking over Misty's shoulder. "That's a really difficult task. Jessica's obviously pony mad and it looks like you'll be visiting her at the stable. Be careful, Misty. Horses are really big and scary. You never know what they're going to do or where they'll put their thumping great hoofs."

Misty laughed.

"Don't worry, Coral. I love animals,

even the big, unpredictable ones. I don't mind meeting Jessica *and* her pony."

Coral was unconvinced. "You'd better check your wand's working before you go," she said.

Misty waved her wand in a circle, giggling as the wand neighed loudly. Blue stars cantered from its tip and formed a shimmering horseshoe in the air. The class cheered and Coral clapped loudly.

"Well done, Misty," said Miss Alaska, smiling. "Off you go then. Good luck with your first task."

Misty's stomach was fizzling like fireworks as she walked out of the class cave. At last she'd been chosen to take her first task and what a brilliant task it was. Animals and making new friends were two of Misty's favourite things. In the playground she perched on a stone bench while she studied the map on the sycamore leaf to see where she was going. Jessica's house backed on to a field with a stable where she kept her pony. Carefully wrapping the leaf round her wand, Misty set out to find her.

Chapter Two

The Main Tunnel was crowded with Fairy
Bears all heading for the Grand Door.
Misty joined them, lightly running her paw
along the jewel-studded wall, loving the feel
of the magically sparkling gem stones. She
queued patiently to climb the gnarled root
staircase, but when her turn finally came
she raced up the steps and through the huge
wooden door that led to the inside of the
sycamore tree. The hollow tree guarded
the entrance to the Crystal Caves, hiding
it from the outside world. Misty stood for

a moment at the
bottom of the
tree enjoying
the darkness
and the soft
humming
sound of
wings as
Fairy
Bears
flew
up the
trunk. Fur
crackling with
excitement
she joined them,
flying up towards
the pale circle of light
shining through the forgotten squirrel
hole and out into Firefly Meadow. Misty

14

breathed in the fresh morning air and
somersaulted with joy.

"Hi, Misty. Are you going on a task?"

Misty looked up and saw Racer, a senior
in Miss Pan's class, waving at her.

"Hi, Racer, I'm going on my *first* task,"
said Misty proudly.

"Good luck." Racer dipped his light
green wings.

Misty couldn't wait to meet Jessica and
get started on her task but she flew steadily,
carefully checking her map to make sure
she was going in the right direction. Jessica
lived in a tiny house with an enormous
garden. At the bottom of the garden,
enclosed by a fence, was a field with a
small stable block, separated by a second
fence. Misty smiled as she flew towards it.
There was Jessica's bike propped against
the fence and there was Becky, sitting

on a hay-bale reading a book.

Misty entered the yard and landed on the fence, hiding behind a post. There was a loud whinny and then the clip clop of hoofs as Jessica led her pony out of the stable. Tying the pony to the fence, Jessica went into the tack room. Moments later she returned, carrying a grooming kit.

"Do you want to help groom Honey?" she called to Becky.

Becky glanced up from her book and shook her head.

"No thanks."

Jessica hesitated but Becky had her nose firmly stuck in her book. Shrugging her shoulders she began grooming her pony. Every now and then she glanced across at Becky and once she opened her mouth as if to speak, but Becky seemed so engrossed in her story that Jessica changed her mind.

When Honey's coat was gleaming, Jessica put the grooming kit away and brought out a saddle and bridle.

"Would you like to help me tack Honey up?" she called.

"No," said Becky, not bothering to look up this time.

"Do you want to come out with me? I'll lead you on Honey if you like or you can ride my bike?"

Becky sighed.

"I'm reading," she said pointedly.

Jessica looked worried. In silence she tacked Honey up then put on her riding hat and tightened the chin strap. Untying Honey from the fence, she led her to the gate.

"I'm going now. Are you sure you'll be all right on your own?" asked Jessica, frowning.

"I'm sure," muttered Becky.

Jessica hesitated before ploughing on.

"I won't be long. I'll just go for a
quick ride and then we can do something
together. You can wait for me in my
secret den if you like. It's up in the hayloft.
There's a ladder outside Honey's stable to
reach it. I haven't been in the den for ages
because of school, but I'm going to now it's
half-term. It's brilliant fun up there!"

Becky pulled a face.

"Is it quiet?" she asked.

"Very," said Jessica.

"I might," she said.

Jessica led Honey out of the yard and
mounted her, waving as she rode away.
Becky didn't wave back. She was too busy
reading.

Misty could hardly believe her ears. She'd
got it all wrong. Poor Jessica! No wonder

she was having trouble making friends with her new stepsister. What was wrong with Becky? Was she always this unfriendly? Misty quickly took off after Jessica, who was riding Honey at a smart trot. Misty's brain whirred as she flew. Jessica had already tried all the things Misty was going to suggest to make friends. What should she do next? It was difficult to find the right moment to show herself to Jessica, who kept Honey going at a fast pace, but eventually she pulled up to give the pony a rest. Immediately Misty flew down and landed on Honey's soft white mane.

"Hello, Jessica. I'm Misty the Fairy Bear. I'm here to help you," Misty introduced herself.

Jessica nearly fell off Honey in surprise and grabbed hold of the saddle.

"A Fairy Bear!" she exclaimed. "I've

never heard of one before. Are you like a
real fairy?"

"Sort of! Fairy Bears use magic to help
look after the world and the creatures and
plants in it," Misty explained.

"That's amazing," said Jessica, unable
to take her eyes off Misty. "But why have
you come to help me? It's Becky that needs
help. Her dad and my mum got married

a little while ago and this is the first time we've spent any time together. I don't think she likes me very much. She never wants to do anything with me."

"That's why I'm here. To help you to get along with Becky." Misty fell silent, not wanting to admit that she wasn't sure where to start.

Jessica's green eyes lit up joyfully.

"Thank you, Misty. I've been so worried about Becky. I can't tell Mum or Mick because they're so happy together and I don't want to spoil it for them. Let's go back to the stable now. Honey will have to make do with a quick ride if it means you can help me make friends with Becky."

Chapter Three

Back at the stables Becky was still sitting on the hay-bale reading her book. Keeping out of sight Misty flew behind her and landed on the fence.

"Hi!" said Jessica cheerfully, jumping off Honey. She ran up her stirrups, opened the gate then led her pony into the yard.

"Didn't you want to read in my den?"

Becky looked up from her book.

"It was too noisy. I couldn't concentrate," she answered.

"Noisy? But the den's really quiet. It's

my secret place. No one knows it's there."
Jessica was baffled.

"It was very noisy up there," argued
Becky. "I kept hearing a funny snoring
sound."

"Snoring?" repeated Jessica. "That's odd.
I'll untack Honey and then I'll take a look.
Do you want to help me?"

"No thanks."

Sighing softly Jessica ran her hand along
Honey's tummy then unbuckled the girth,
the long strap holding the saddle in place.
She looped it over the saddle's seat and
lifted the whole thing from her pony's back.

Misty watched in fascination until a
horsefly buzzed past so close that she nearly
toppled off the fence.

"Watch out," she called, even though
the horsefly couldn't understand her cross
words. It flew towards Honey who swished

her tail at it. The horsefly
neatly dodged out of the way then flew at
Honey again. Irritated Honey kicked out.

"Steady," soothed Jessica. She swapped
Honey's bridle for a head collar and lead
rope and tied her to the fence.

The horsefly lunged again, deftly landing
on Honey's back and biting her on her
rump.

"Neigh!" squealed Honey, bucking with pain.

Instantly Jessica was at Honey's head, holding on to her head collar and talking to her in a calm voice.

Honey stopped bucking and her ears twitched as she listened to Jessica's softly spoken words, but she was trembling badly.

"Steady, girl." Jessica ran her hand down Honey's golden neck until she had stopped shaking.

Misty fluttered her wings, soaring high in the air to avoid being seen by Becky, and landed on Jessica's hand. Jessica caught her breath in delight.

"Honey was bitten by a horsefly," Misty explained. "Their bite really stings. Shall I use some Fairy Bear magic to make it better?"

"So that's what happened! Thank you,

Misty." Jessica was very grateful.

Raising her wand, Misty pointed it at Honey's bottom and chanted.

"Bright stars glow,
Make the pain go."

Her gold wand trembled as a flurry of tiny blue stars burst from the end and fell on to Honey. Hissing and popping, the stars dissolved.

Honey looked round. It was obvious that the pain had gone as she snorted her thanks to Misty.

On the other side of the yard Becky stood up and slipped through the gate. Jessica called to her, asking her to stay but Becky shook her head.

"It's too noisy," she said, stomping across the field towards the house.

Jessica's mouth drooped.

"I really don't think she likes me."

"Something's bothering her, but it can't be you," said Misty thoughtfully.

Misty thought about Becky as she watched Jessica remove Honey's tack and get the dirt off her pony using a large brush. But she couldn't think of a reason why Becky was so unfriendly.

"The tack room and feed store is a bit of a mess," said Jessica, putting the brush away. "I keep meaning to tidy it but I've been so busy at school this term."

Misty stared at the L-shaped room. The

front part, where Jessica kept the things she needed for Honey, was very tidy, but the bit at the back behind the feed bins was full of junk.

"Can I see your den?" Misty asked.

Jessica brightened.

"Follow me," she said, leading the way along a wide corridor to Honey's stable. In contrast to the tack room the stable was clean and bright with a fresh bed of straw, a clean bucket of water and a hay net hanging on the wall.

"See up there." Jessica pointed to a square hole in the roof, just outside the stable, with a sturdy ladder leading up to it. "That's the hayloft. My den's up there."

Carefully, holding on to the handrail, she climbed up the ladder and disappeared inside the hole. Misty flew after her and stared around in amazement. The hayloft

was much larger than
she'd imagined,
with sloping
walls and a
hole at one end.
Sunlight poured
through the
hole, shining
on to a neatly
stacked pile of hay-
bales. The smell was
wonderful. Misty took a
deep breath, loving the sweet scent of hay
mingled with the smell of warm horse. In
one corner Jessica had arranged the hay-
bales to make a room. Inside there was a
squashy beanbag and an old wooden crate
turned over to make a cupboard. The roof
was too low for Jessica to stand up properly
so she crawled towards it.

"This is my den. Here's my favourite
mug with a picture of a horse like Honey
on it." Jessica reached into the box and held
up the mug for Misty to see. "Mum gives
me juice and . . ."

She broke off suddenly, her eyes wide
with surprise.

"Did you hear that?"

Misty nodded. She'd heard the strange yapping noise too.

"There it is again," whispered Jessica.

Something was snoring, snuffling and yapping in the opposite corner to the den. Jessica slowly crept towards it with Misty flying alongside her. The strange noises sounded familiar. Misty's brain buzzed as she tried to remember where she'd heard those sounds before. All at once she knew what it was. Flying in front of Jessica's face she raised a tiny paw.

"Stop!" she whispered.

Jessica pulled up in surprise, but before Misty could explain Jessica saw for herself.

"A nest!" she exclaimed.

In the corner of the roof, nestled in a broken bale of straw, was a barn owl. Her black eyes stared warily out from her

beautiful
heart-
shaped face.
Yapping
and snuffling
in the hay
around her
were three
owlets. Jessica
gave a soft
gasp of delight.

"They're so sweet," she mouthed.

Misty loved baby animals, and barn-
owl chicks were particularly cute. They
looked like enormous balls of fluffy white
wool. One of the chicks was braver than
the rest and stuck his head forward, peering
at Jessica and Misty with huge inquisitive
eyes. The mother owl gave a sharp warning
screech and her owlet pulled back. So did

Jessica and Misty. Quickly and quietly
they moved away from the owl's nest, not
speaking until they were safely down the
ladder and back in the stable block.

"So that's who was making the strange
noises that Becky heard," said Jessica, her
green eyes sparkling. "We won't be able to
use my den for a while in case we frighten
them."

"That's right," Misty agreed. "Mother
birds sometimes abandon their nests if
they're disturbed."

"The baby birds are so sweet. I bet even
Becky would love to see them. Do you
think it would be all right if I brought her
up here? We'll be very quiet and we'll only
come the once."

"It'll be fine," said Misty, hoping that a
shared secret of the baby owls would bring
the two girls closer together.

"Let's go and get her right now," said Jessica enthusiastically.

Jessica could hardly contain her excitement. She untied Honey and turned her out in the field. She ran so fast from the field to her house that Misty's blue wings were a blur as she sped after her new friend. Bursting through the back door of the house Jessica found Becky making a jewellery box at the kitchen table. Misty flew inside and hid in a pot of herbs growing on the window sill.

basil

"Becky, come quickly," panted Jessica. "I've got something really exciting to show you."

"What?" asked Becky, concentrating on sticking a shell on the box's lid.

"There's an owl's nest in my den. There are three of the cutest owlets you've ever seen and you should hear them. That's why it was so noisy up there. They make the funniest snoring sound ever."

Becky wiped glue from her fingers before picking up another shell. She didn't even bother to look at Jessica.

"I'm busy right now," she said.

Jessica's excitement vanished.

"Well, if you're too busy . . ." her voice trailed away.

"I am," Becky said firmly. She kept her head bent over the jewellery box, making it clear that the conversation was finished.

Misty nearly jumped out of her hiding
place with frustration. What was wrong
with Becky? Why was she being so mean?
Raising her wand Misty pointed it straight
at Becky's wavy brown hair.

"These friendship stars are just for you.
Make a new friend and be a friend too."

The wand hissed and grew warm in Misty's paw. The sapphire lit up and then, in a flash of blue, a sparkling stream of stars cascaded from the end. But Misty was too far away from Becky and the stars missed her! They landed in a starry puddle on the kitchen floor and melted away.

Jessica looked round in surprise, but Becky hadn't noticed at all. Feeling foolish, Misty lowered her wand. Now she thought about it, perhaps friendship stars weren't the right sort of magic to fix this problem. Her task had been to help Jessica, not Becky. It was all so confusing! Glumly, Misty realized she was stuck. She had no idea how to help Jessica make friends with prickly Becky.

Chapter Four

Promising Jessica she would return, Misty
flew back to the Crystal Caves. It was a
lovely day, bright sunshine with a light
breeze, but Misty didn't notice. She was
too wrapped up in working out a way to
help Jessica. She flew over Firefly Meadow,
hardly seeing the colourful flowers growing
amongst the grass as she headed towards
the sycamore tree. Misty flew through the
squirrel hole and down the dark insides.
How should she solve this impossible
task? Whichever way Misty looked at the

problem she always came back to the same answer.

"It's not Jessica who needs help making friends, it's Becky!" she said in exasperation.

Misty liked Jessica. She was kind and fun to be with. She couldn't understand what Becky's problem was. Misty's wings trembled with frustration as she landed at the bottom of the tree trunk, fluttering through the Grand Door and down the gnarled root staircase. If she didn't come up with an answer soon, she would fail Jessica and her task!

"I'm so stuck," said Misty miserably.

"Talking to yourself?" Racer came through the Grand Door and hopped down the staircase.

"Hi, Racer." Misty managed a small smile. "I can't work out how to solve my task."

"Do you want to tell me about it?" Racer asked.

"Yes, please," said Misty gratefully. Misty always shared her problems. She found it helped to talk things over with her friends or her mum and dad.

Racer sat on the bottom step, patting the root for Misty to join him. Although Racer was a senior he was a good friend to everyone, and Misty didn't feel shy in his company. She sat down, neatly folding her wings behind her back, and began explaining the problem of Jessica and Becky.

"It's not Jessica's fault that Becky won't make friends," she finished. "Jessica is trying really hard to be nice."

"That's a difficult problem," said Racer, tapping his wand against his paw. "Maybe Becky's shy?"

"Or maybe she doesn't find it as easy to make friends as you both do," said Miss Alaska.

Misty Makes Friends

Misty and Racer jumped. They hadn't seen Miss Alaska coming along the Main Tunnel.

"You're very lucky. You're both easy-going and always have something to say, but not everyone is like that. Lots of Fairy Bears and people get tongue-tied when in company. They say the wrong thing or worse still can't think of anything to say."

Miss Alaska smiled at the surprised looks on Misty and Racer's faces.

"Or maybe there's something that's stopping Becky from making friends with Jessica," Miss Alaska continued. "Perhaps you should concentrate on getting to know Becky better."

"That's a good idea." Misty jumped to her paws. "I'll start right now."

"It's too late to go out now," said Miss Alaska, laughing at Misty's enthusiasm.

"You can try again tomorrow. Aren't you supposed to be meeting some of your own friends after school?"

Misty had been so wrapped up in her task she'd forgotten about her trip to the underground lake. It was a good thing Miss Alaska had reminded her.

"Thanks, Miss Alaska, and thanks, Racer." Misty wiggled her wings to say goodbye.

As she flew along the Grand Tunnel, Coral sped by in the opposite direction. Misty slowed and called out, "Hi, Coral, are you sure you can't come to the lake with us?"

Coral slowed then came back, hovering alongside Misty.

"Thanks, Misty. I'd really love to but
I promised to help Mum so I'd better not.
How was your task and how was that big
scary horse?"

"Not scary at all," laughed Misty. "But I
haven't finished my task yet."

"Good luck then," said Coral, flying on
her way.

Coral's words kept replaying in Misty's
head. Coral was scared of horses. Misty
didn't think she was scared of anything, but
she knew of things that frightened other
Fairy Bears. What about Becky? Was
something scaring her and stopping her
from making friends with Jessica? Could
that be why she seemed so unfriendly?

Misty had a great time playing with her
friends at the underground lake. First they
flew over to Rocky Island to admire the

45

jewel-encrusted rocks. Then they flew back
and sat on the shore, dipping their paws
in the shimmering blue water to catch
the rainbow-coloured fish swimming in
the shallows. But even the magical lake
couldn't stop Misty from thinking about
Becky. The more she thought about it the
more convinced she grew that Becky *was*
scared of something. Misty couldn't wait for
the following day when she could meet up
with the girls again and carry on with her
task.

"Wake up, Misty." Primrose tickled her
in the ribs. "I asked if you wanted a rowing
race but you were miles away."

"I was," said Misty. "Ooh, stop it. That
tickles!" Giggling happily she turned and
tickled Primrose back.

"Do you want to race or not?" laughed
Primrose when they finally fell apart.

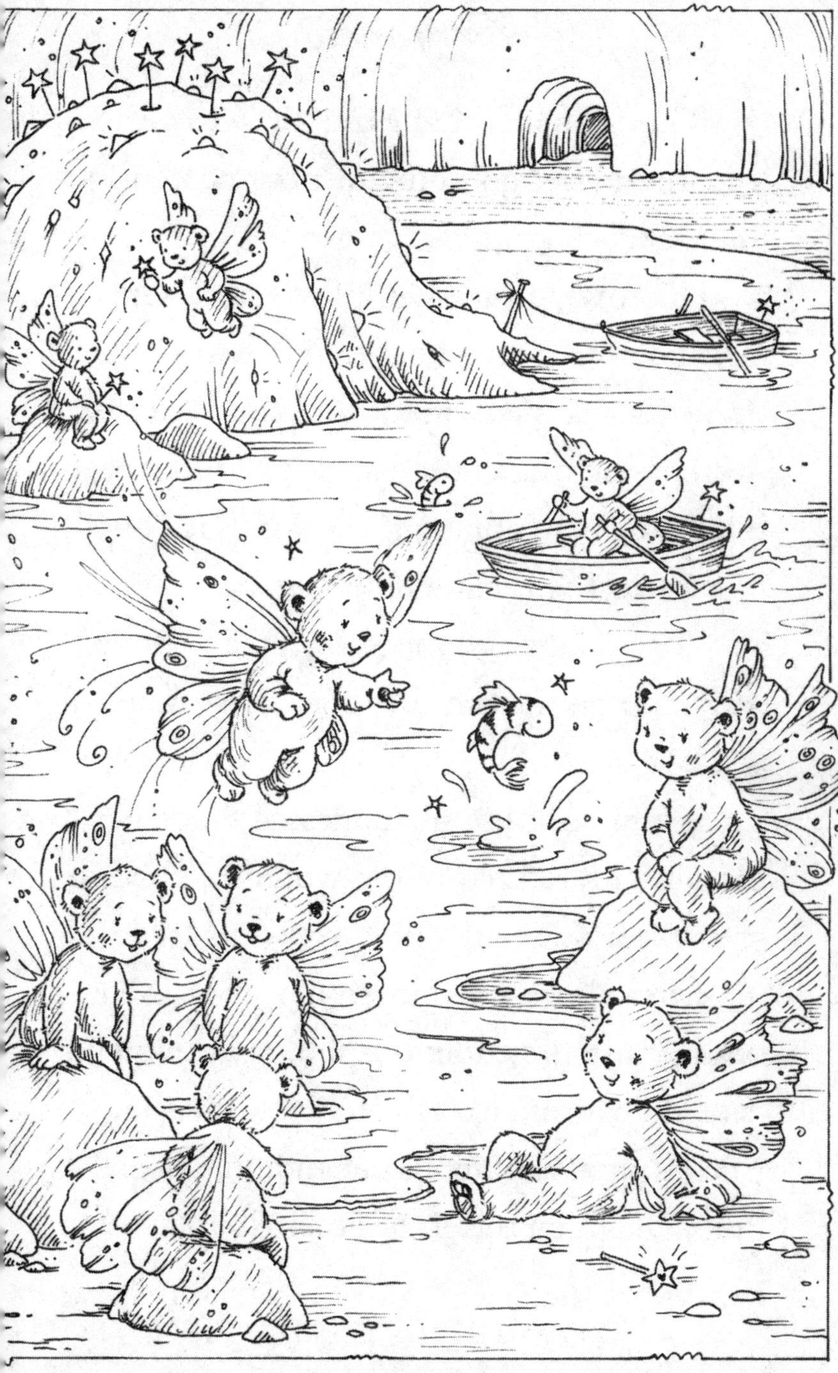

"Go on then," said Misty. "One race and then I'd better go home. It must be nearly teatime."

The rowing race was fun to start with. Misty chose a blue boat and Primrose a green one. Lulu, Sunny and Dizzy wanted to race too and chose violet, yellow and lilac boats. Swapping their wands for oars the Fairy Bears climbed aboard.

"It's once round the lake," called Poppy, standing on the shore. "One, two, three, GO!"

Sporty Lulu got away first, her oars dipping in and out of the water so fast you could hardly see them. Next was Misty, closely followed by Sunny and Dizzy, with Primrose trailing behind. Misty knew she had no chance of catching Lulu, but she thought she might get second place. She pulled harder on her oars, smiling

triumphantly as the gap between herself
and Sunny widened.

"Hurray!" cried Poppy from the shore.
"Lulu wins. And in second place it's going
to be Misty."

Misty pulled harder, determined to beat
Sunny who was rapidly catching up. Then
suddenly her oars missed the water and she
toppled backwards in the boat. She put out
her paws to save herself and accidentally
dropped both oars. With a loud splash the
oars went overboard.

Misty sat up quickly and leaned over
the side, trying to rescue the oars, but they
had drifted out of reach. The boat rocked
violently as she stretched a little further.
Misty stopped reaching for the oars and sat
still until the boat stopped wobbling.

"Careful, Misty," called Poppy.

Misty waved a paw. She knew the boat

couldn't capsize, but now that she didn't
have any oars the rocking sensation scared
her. Misty glanced longingly at her wand
propped up against a stone on the shore.
If only she had it with her now, she could

rescue the oars with magic. Trying not
to let the fear take control of her Misty
wondered how she was going to reach the
shore.

Chapter Five

The boat tilted more violently as Sunny rowed nearer. Misty paled and gripped the seat with both paws. This was scary. She tensed her wings and closed her eyes, waiting for Sunny to pass her and claim second place.

"Misty, throw me the rope."

Sunny was calling to her. Surprised, Misty opened her eyes and saw that, instead of overtaking, Sunny had pulled alongside her boat.

"Throw me the mooring rope and I'll

tow you ashore," called Sunny, fluttering her yellow wings.

Misty didn't want to reach for the rope in case the boat rocked even harder than it was already.

"Come on, Misty, you can do it!" encouraged Dizzy.

Misty took a deep calming breath. She could do this. She just had to be brave.

"Misty."

Misty looked round and saw Lulu rowing towards her with the lost oars.

"Are these yours?" she called cheekily.

Misty laughed with delight. There was nothing to be afraid of. All her friends had come to her rescue. She could even hear Poppy shouting encouragement from the shore. Leaning forward, Misty reached out and threw the rope to Sunny who immediately began towing her to the land. They were met by Lulu who passed the lost oars across the water to Misty.

"She doesn't need them now. She's got us!" said Sunny, laughing.

A warm feeling, from the bottom of her paws to the tips of her ears, seeped over Misty. What fantastic friends she had. Surrounded by a flotilla of boats Misty came ashore.

That night Misty slept so well that she almost *over*slept. Luckily her parents woke her up, as Dad had to go out early

too. Together
they flew to
the Grand
Door, up
the hollow
trunk and
out through
the squirrel
hole.

"Good luck,"
said Dad, kissing Misty goodbye.

"Thanks, Dad."

Misty flew all the way to Jessica's
without stopping. It was too early for the
girls to be awake but Honey had spent
the night in her stable and she snorted a
friendly greeting as Misty flew in to see
her. Misty looked around for somewhere
to wait for Jessica. Deciding that the
stable wasn't a good hiding place she flew

upward, meaning to wait just inside the trapdoor to Jessica's secret den. But as Misty grew closer she heard a scuffling noise followed by a loud yap and then a bump. Curiously she flew through the trapdoor to see what all the noise was about. Misty hovered in the air, trying not to laugh. The owlets were learning to fly. They bumped around the hayloft flapping their fluffy wings, fluttering a few paces before crash landing with a thump.

"Shoo!" Misty flew in front of the boldest owlet, who was heading for the trapdoor, ushering him back.

"Yip!" said the bird indignantly.

A shiver ran across Misty's pretty blue wings. This was a dangerous time for the owlets. She hoped they learned to fly quickly, without hurting themselves.

It wasn't long before Misty heard Jessica

cheerfully chatting away to Becky as she
approached the stables. Misty couldn't
wait to see her new friend again. She flew
down into the stable but kept close to the
roof, waiting for an opportunity to speak
to Jessica on her own. The two girls came

inside. Becky had a face like a stormy day and answered Jessica's questions with one-word grunts.

"What's wrong? You sound upset," said Jessica kindly.

"I didn't want to come to the stables today. I wanted to stay indoors, but your mum wouldn't let me," said Becky.

Jessica flushed with embarrassment, "Sorry about that. Mum has this thing about fresh air being good for you. We'll go inside later. I'll help you with your jewellery box if you like?"

"It's finished," said Becky quickly.

"OK, well why don't you come for a ride with me then?" coaxed Jessica warmly. "We can take turns on Honey. It'll be great fun."

"I don't want to go for a ride. I'm going to read instead," said Becky.

Suddenly her face fell.

"Oh no! I've left my book indoors. I bet your mum won't let me go and get it."

"Mum's not like that," said Jessica. "Of course she'll let you get your book."

Becky looked uncertain.

"How about if I go and get it?" asked Jessica. "Is it the one you were reading last night?"

"Yes." Becky nodded gratefully. "I left it in my bedroom."

"I'll be two ticks," said Jessica, hanging Honey's head collar and lead rein over the stable door.

She sprinted out of the stable, leaving Becky awkwardly hanging around in the corridor. From her hiding place on the ceiling Misty watched her. Becky's face was pinched white, as if she was worried about something. Misty wondered if she should

go and
talk to
her, but
before she
could make
up her mind
there was a loud
scuffling noise from the
hayloft. Misty glanced over
and saw the biggest owlet peering out of
the trapdoor. She gasped. The bird wasn't
ready to fly. The owlet seemed to think so
too. He backed away from the trapdoor
and disappeared from view. Misty sighed
with relief. That had been close. But a
few seconds later he was back, his big eyes
peering curiously at the space beneath him.

"Go back," hissed Misty, flying towards
him.

Gripping on with his large claws the

owlet leaned out further. Misty groaned. He wouldn't have understood her words. She flew faster, knowing she had to reach the bird before he fell.

Suddenly the owlet leaned too far. With a startled screech he toppled forward, his fluffy wings flapping frantically. He managed to fly a few strokes before his wings gave up and he spiralled out of control.

There was nothing Misty could do to save him. Her magic wasn't strong enough. She watched in dismay, wincing as the tiny bird fell to the ground. Incredibly he landed in a pile of straw in Honey's stable. Misty's breath huffed out in relief. Thank goodness the bird hadn't landed on the concrete floor in the corridor outside. That would have really hurt! But the owlet wasn't out of danger yet.

"No!" Becky's hand flew to her mouth as she too saw the baby owl fall.

If Honey stepped backwards, she would tread on the tiny bird. Misty stared down in horror. Becky stood very still, her face white, then slowly she picked up Honey's head collar and lead rein and went inside the stable. At first Misty thought that Becky didn't want to scare the bird, but as she watched the girl nervously creep across the stable she realized that Becky was terrified of Honey. Her hands were trembling and her voice shook as she called for the pony

to stand still. So that was why Becky had
been so unfriendly! Just like Coral, Becky
was scared of horses. After the incident in
the rowing boat Misty understood how she
felt. When Becky was an arm's length from
Honey, she reached out and looped the
head collar over the pony's face. It took her

a while to get the straps in the right position because she was standing too far away.

"Move closer," Misty whispered under her breath.

At last the head collar was in place. Keeping one eye on the baby owl Becky's fingers fumbled with the buckle. Misty could hardly bear to watch. If Becky didn't hurry up, Honey might step back and crush the bird.

Chapter Six

Becky was too frightened to move quickly.
Clumsily her fingers worked at Honey's
head collar. It was time to lend a paw.
Raising her wand Misty pointed it at
Honey's hoofs as she prepared to cast a spell
to stop the pony from moving her feet and
stepping on the owl. But as she began to
recite the magic words Becky pulled herself
together.

Voice trembling she said, "Walk on."

Honey twitched an ear.

"Walk on," said Becky more firmly.

Obediently Honey moved forward and with a small sigh of relief Becky led the horse out of the stable and into the yard. Misty flew after her. It took ages for Becky to tie the pony up and when she'd finished she collapsed on a nearby hay-bale.

"Becky, what happened? Why are you shaking and why is Honey in the yard?"

Misty Makes Friends

Jessica came running towards the fence.

"Come and see," said Becky, managing a small smile.

Dumping Becky's book on the hay-bale, Jessica followed her into the stable. Unseen by both of the girls, Misty went with them.

"Oh!" exclaimed Jessica when she saw the baby bird flapping around in the stable. "How did it get down there?"

Becky explained how the owlet had fallen through the trapdoor and how she'd had to move Honey to prevent the pony from stepping on it.

"Well done! That was smart of you," said Jessica.

Becky blushed and Misty waited for her to explain how terrified she was of horses, but to her surprise Becky didn't

mention it. Instead she asked, "What shall we do about the bird? Shall we put it back in the hayloft?"

Jessica shook her head.

"You're not supposed to touch baby birds or their parents might abandon them. We might have to leave it here. I'll go and ask Mum. She'll know what to do. Will you look after Honey for me? She'll be fine tied up in the yard, but I'd feel happier if someone was with her."

"Er . . ." Becky hesitated.

"I won't be long," called Jessica, already jogging back to the house. Misty sped after her and when they were out of Becky's sight she flew down and landed on Jessica's nose.

Jessica skidded to a halt and Misty almost fell off. She fluttered into the air and landed on Jessica's hand.

Misty Makes Friends

"Hello," said Jessica, beaming at Misty. "You'll never guess what happened."

"I know," said Misty, quickly explaining how she'd been hiding in the stable all along.

"I never saw you!" Jessica was impressed.

"Fairy Bears are good at hiding, and I think I know why Becky has been so unfriendly." Misty explained to Jessica how scared Becky was of horses and how difficult it had been for her to move Honey.

"So that's why she was shaking!" said Jessica. "I couldn't work that out. Poor

Becky! Why didn't she tell me?"

"Maybe she was too embarrassed. Why don't you ask her?" said Misty, remembering how talking to Racer and Miss Alaska had helped her.

"I will, when I've asked Mum about the baby owl. I'd better hurry, seeing as Becky is scared of horses."

Misty rode on Jessica's shoulder, hidden by her blonde hair, as Jessica went indoors. Mum was in the kitchen making cookies for lunch.

"You mustn't touch the owlet," she said, stirring the cookie mixture. "The parents will be nearby and they'll feed the owl until it's strong enough to fly. It's lucky it fell into Honey's stable. If it had been outside it might have been caught by a cat or a fox."

"This means I'll have to leave Honey in the field at night," said Jessica.

"She'll be fine outside. The nights are quite warm," Mum reassured her.

On the way back to the stables Jessica worried about how to talk to Becky, now she knew she was afraid of horses.

"She doesn't like me. I bet that's why she didn't want me to know. Maybe I won't ask her about it," she said.

"Becky was very brave when she led Honey out of the stable. Now it's your turn to be brave. You have to talk to her," urged Misty.

Jessica sighed.

"You're right."

"I'll be here with you," Misty continued.

"Sitting on my shoulder? Thanks, Misty. That'll give me loads of courage." Jessica brightened immediately.

Misty wasn't surprised to find Becky sitting far away from Honey with her nose buried inside her book. She was so engrossed she didn't notice Jessica until she sat down beside her. Taking a deep breath Jessica came straight out with her question, asking Becky if she was scared of horses.

Becky face flushed a deep shade of scarlet.

"What if I am?" she asked, her voice suddenly prickly.

"Becky, you're so brave!" Impulsively Jessica hugged her stepsister. "If I was scared of horses I could never have done what you did to rescue that baby owl."

"I bet you would have," mumbled Becky, looking down at the floor.

"Why didn't you tell me before? It must have been horrible being dragged down to the stables every day."

"It was too embarrassing. I thought you'd call me a wimp. I was really excited when Dad said he was marrying your mum and I'd be getting a new stepsister. He didn't mention anything about a horse until I got here."

"He probably thought it would be a lovely surprise," said Jessica kindly.

"Your dad loves surprises."

Hidden by Jessica's hair, Misty's wings twitched joyfully. She'd done it! She'd finally helped Jessica and Becky start to become friends. But, just to be sure, Misty raised her wand and chanted,

"Make friends, make friends,
Never ever break friends.
Friends care, friends share,
Good friends are always there."

Dramatically pointing her wand at the two girls Misty held it tightly as a stream of blue stars burst out from the end. The stars landed over Jessica and Becky before dissolving.

"What was that?" said Becky, touching her hair.

Catching sight of a lone blue star as it

fizzled to nothing Jessica said with a smile, "There must be a little magic in the air."

Chapter Seven

"Do you believe in magic? So do I!" Becky smiled back.

"Do you want to have a ride on Honey?" asked Jessica suddenly. "I'd lead you and I'd go really slowly."

Becky laughed.

"I'm not ready for that. But we could make a new den, seeing as we can't use your old one for a while."

"That's an excellent idea," said Jessica. "We could make one behind the feed bins. I've been meaning to clear that space out

for ages. I'll turn Honey out into the field
and then we'll get started."

Misty was delighted that Jessica and
Becky were getting on so well and thrilled
that she'd passed her task. When Becky
was looking the other way, she flew from
Jessica's shoulder. It was time to go but
she couldn't leave without saying a
proper goodbye.
She knew
Jessica felt the
same because
she put
her hand
to her
shoulder
and looked
really sad when Misty
wasn't there. Misty had completed her task
too well. Becky was keen to show Jessica

what a good friend she was and stuck to her like glue. Misty wondered if she should let Becky see her but decided against it. Jessica and Becky were having great fun clearing out the tack and feed room to make a new den and Misty didn't want to interfere.

"Did you know there's a window back here?" Becky moved a stack of old feed bags and stared at the dusty window in surprise.

"I'd forgotten," admitted Jessica bashfully.

"It's covered in cobwebs but if we clean them off it'll let more light in. We might be able to watch the adult owls hunting for their owlets," said Becky excitedly.

"Eeek!" Jessica jumped back in alarm.

"What's wrong?" asked Becky.

"A spider!" Jessica took another step backwards. "Erm, I'll go and get Mum."

"Why?" said Becky, reaching forward and gently catching the spider in her hand. "It's only little. I'll put it outside."

"How can you do that?" said Jessica when Becky returned. "I hate spiders. They're so scary."

"You're scared of spiders?" Becky stared at Jessica in amazement and then she began to laugh.

"What?" asked Jessica.

"You," said Becky, shaking with laughter. "A little spider is nowhere near as scary as an enormous horse."

"I don't like their legs." Jessica shuddered.

Then laughing she added, "But I see what you mean."

"I'll go and get a bucket of water to clean the cobwebs off the window," said Becky.

"Thanks," said Jessica gratefully. "I'll carry on tidying stuff while you're gone."

The moment Becky left the tack room Misty quickly fluttered over to Jessica.

"You're still here!" Jessica was delighted.

"I couldn't leave without saying goodbye," said Misty.

"Goodbye then," said Jessica. "I'm going to miss you, but at least I've got Becky now. I think we're going to be really good friends."

There was one last thing Misty wanted to do before she went home. Twirling her wand in the air she recited the Fairy Bear friendship spell.

Misty Makes Friends

"From me to you,
A star that's true!"

Warmth flooded through her wand and it
almost jumped out of Misty's paw
as a large blue star burst from its
tip. It took two paws to
hold it. Carefully Misty
handed the
glittering star
to Jessica.

"It's a
friendship star,"
she explained,
looking up at Jessica.

Jessica took the star
and laid it in the palm of her hand.

"It's the most beautiful thing I've ever
seen," she whispered. A funny expression
crossed her face.

81

"Misty, would you mind if I gave Becky this friendship star? She's been so brave. I really think she deserves it."

"That's a lovely idea," said Misty. Then she had a good idea too. Waving her wand in the air she repeated the friendship spell, laughing at Jessica's surprise as a second blue star burst from her wand.

"One each," she said, handing the new star to Jessica.

Misty Makes Friends

"Thank you, Misty." Jessica stretched out a finger and gently touched Misty's paw.

"Bye, Jessica," said Misty. "Good luck with the den and remember to watch out for the baby owls."

Misty fluttered into the air, waving her wand as she flew away. For a moment she felt sad to be leaving her new friend so suddenly. But remembering all her old friends waiting for her back at the Crystal Caves, Misty somersaulted with delight. She couldn't wait to get home and tell them how she'd finally managed to complete her task. Everyone would be so thrilled for her. Misty's spirits soared as she fluttered homewards through the sunny blue sky.

Misty

1. Favourite colour – *blue*

2. Favourite gemstone – *sapphire*

3. Best flower – *bluebell*

4. Cutest animal – *tiger cub*

5. Birthday month – *May*

6. Yummiest food – *honey surprise*

7. Favourite place – *Starlight Cave*

8. Hobbies – *drawing*

9. Best ever season – *winter*

10. Worst thing – *unhappiness*

Misty's Wordsearch

Looking after a horse is really good fun, but it's also a lot of responsibility and hard work. Help me to find all the words hiding in the puzzle! The words can be up, down, backwards, forwards or even diagonal!

RIDING✓   BOOTS✓   NEIGH   HAY
HONEY   SADDLE   GROOMING
JODHPURS   REINS   STABLE

H	H	B	R	S	A	T	O
G	I	O	H	E	K	J	A
I	D	O	N	U	H	O	G
E	S	T	I	E	A	D	N
N	T	S	O	I	Y	H	I
S	A	D	D	L	E	P	M
O	B	A	S	G	H	U	O
D	L	P	K	M	T	R	O
R	E	I	N	S	J	S	R
L	G	R	I	D	I	N	G

Dizzy Dives In!

Dizzy is in a spin! She has two
problems to solve, but only
enough magic for one.
Will she make the right decision?

Sunny's Surprise

Friendly Fairy Bear Sunny sees
Ella looking sad in her magic mirror.
Sunny promises to cheer Ella up,
but how will she find her?